The Vegetable War

The Vegetable War

by

NAOMI MITCHISON

Illustrated by Polly Loxton

HAMISH HAMILTON

LONDON

First published in Great Britain 1980 by
Hamish Hamilton Children's Books Limited
Garden House, 57-59 Long Acre, London WC2E 9JZ

British Library Cataloguing in Publication Data

Mitchison, Naomi
   The vegetable war.-(Antelope books).
   I. Title   II. Series
   823'.9'1J   PZ7.M699

   ISBN 0-241-10444-0

Printed in Great Britain by Ebenezer Baylis & Son Ltd,
The Trinity Press, Worcester, and London.

(For Charlotte and Martin, who know what really happened)

PRINCIPLES OF ZAMBIAN HUMANISM

1. MAN - CENTREDNESS
2. COMMUNALISM AND MUTUAL AID
3. NON-EXPLOITATION OF MAN-BY-MAN
4. RESPECT FOR HUMAN DIGNITY
5. SELF RELIANCE · HARD WORK
6. RESPECT FOR THE AGED AND INFIRM
7. CO-OPERATIVE
8. INCLUSIVENESS EGALITARIANISM
9. THE EXTENDED FAMILY SYSTEM
10. PATRIOTISM AND RESPECT
11. RECIPROCAL OBLIGATION

1. At Chunga

WHEN ZINGOZI GOT back from school on Friday afternoon, he was tired and thirsty. He stayed with his grandmother in Matero for the whole week. There was no school yet at Chunga, though there was a concrete foundation already and next year, maybe, there would be walls and a roof and a teacher. But it was a long walk home from Matero and Zingozi wanted a cool drink. His little brother was sitting on the ground, trying to make a wire truck, but he was not strong enough to twist the wires right.

"Kangwa, is there food?" Zingozi asked.

"Our mother has gone with a big basket filled with green mealies to sell. With Jelita."

"When will they be back? Is there water?"

There was water right enough, in the

shade of the house, but not enough. When his father came back from the garden more would be needed. Zingozi took a big, comforting drink and then went off to the bore hole and pumped a bucket full, grumbling to himself. When Jelita was old enough, she must do this. It would have been easy for him to get irrigation water from the furrow where it ran so cold and nice, but if anyone saw him doing that, oh they would be angry!

Back at home he put his reading book up

on the shelf; he was tired of it, he had seen all the pictures; but it was his only one. Then he looked in the big pot: cold nzima – porridge. In the little pot: cold stew, beans mostly. He dug a couple of fingers full out of each pot – no dinner for a young hero back from

learning at school and already doing bigger sums than his father! But it would have to do until the women came back. Anyway he must now go down to the garden.

His father was hoeing steadily between the rows of cabbages. He had sold some that morning. There were always customers coming, though some only wanted a penny-worth of leaves to go with the stew and nzima. The sooner he got rid of the cabbages the better, for the crawlers were chewing them up in spite of the spraying – big crickets, caterpillars, every kind of small enemy. But he still had beets, beans, carrots, tomatoes, squash and a few onions left. And along the borders of his acre, sugar cane, mulberries, mangoes and pawpaws, their roots taking in the leakage from the water furrow. Over the last two weeks the sugar cane had shot up, soon it would be time to sell.

Zingozi's father Gitambi had come out from Lusaka; he had been working in a shop and it had shut down. There was no other job to be found. He heard about the Chunga irrigation scheme from talk at the bus stop – fifteen, twenty gardens, water all the year round from the big sewage works, but made clean – strange, that! Not too far out, easy to get one's stuff marketed. He went to a meeting, cautiously, and put his hand up.

Gitambi's father had come from a village and grown crops just like everyone else before the family moved into the big city, just before Independence, hoping for great things, they didn't know what. How they'd all shouted and cheered! But in spite of Independence and all the cheering he never found a good job, he wasn't educated, he didn't understand city things. So Gitambi was back where he had started, hoeing, hoeing. There was one big snag to the scheme. Every man who came in had to make his share of the water furrow. Day after day, taking the earth from the storm-water ditch which caught the heavy rains from the hills at the other side of the road, they carried it across and built up the walls of the water furrow, so that the irrigation water was always just higher than the gardens. That was hard. It went on and on with no pay, rewarded by thinking all the time that it would be theirs in the end.

To begin with they had lived in a grass-

thatched clay hut and made do with pennies from charcoal burning. They lived poor that first year. Gitambi's wife was good all the same, she made jokes all the time, and managed to make stews with a handful of beans and a few wild roots and leaves. Some of the men who held up their hands fell out, they couldn't take it. But Zingozi's father worked and worked, and then, all at once, there were seeds, they came up, there was a garden. His own garden, an acre, and all the water he needed, any time. His own garden!

"Zingozi, take the other hoe. These weeds must go."

It was heavy, that hoe, all iron. Zingozi did a few strokes, jabbing it into the heavy clay soil and pulling it back.

"Father, I am only just back from school. I have not eaten."

His father said nothing for a time, grunted, stood back and said, "Your mother went with the mealies. She should have taken cabbages as well. When she comes back, we will eat."

"I am hungry now," said Zingozi.

"I have been hungry many times," Gitambi said. "Finish the cabbages. I must do the beets."

But at last, there was his mother, walking proudly, her new head scarf tied in a jaunty bow. Jelita pulled back, grizzling; she didn't like having to wear her pink town dress, it was tight round the neck. They went up to the hut. In a while his mother waved and shouted. Zingozi dropped the hoe and hurried. His mother had blown up the fire and now the stew smelled good. She had stirred up the meat from the bottom and put in bits of sausage.

"Wait!" she said.

When Zingozi started to complain she popped a big sucking sweet into his mouth; that meant she had done well. It was time to eat; his father must be served first. Zingozi's mother dished out a great plate full of the stew, stood beside her man, watched him eat for a minute, and then took out the money from the tight fold of her head scarf and

poured out the jingling coins. "Twelve ngwee each for my mealie cobs, except for those very small ones and for them I charged five!"

"Did you go to the depot like I said?" his father asked her while she made the money into little piles and he watched them grow. Zingozi was scraping his plate, hoping for more.

"Not me!" his mother said. "They would give me only seven ngwee, or maybe eight. I go to my own corner by the roundabout. There is plenty of room, plenty of customers, and trees where Jelita can play safely. Ladies driving smart cars come there wanting five, six mealie cobs. Ministers' wives, they might be. Look, my husband, where this money goes. I've got tea, a tin of meat, oil and matches. But there is still so much we want: blankets, curtains for windows, a new stove for me to cook really well. Glasses for when your friends come –"

"I want –," Jelita began, but Zingozi pinched her and she shut up.

Father said, "Maybe a goat kid? There is grass now."

"But who is to herd?" his wife said. "I cannot chase a goat all the time. And Zingozi is away at school."

"Maybe Jelita –"

But Jelita set up a howl. "Don't like goats."

"We will put the money away in the Credit Union," said father decidedly. "It will be safe there. Then at the end of the season we shall see. Maybe I should get a sprayer for myself. I can't always have the one we all use and the bugs eat my plants too much. Seeds. Fertiliser." He picked up the money, then gave back thirty ngwee; Zingozi's mother knew this was for herself, something for the house or a piece of stuff to make an apron. "Maybe we'll get the stove," he said. "But first we must get the loan for a better house, two rooms, an iron roof, if this selling goes well." And then he added, "But you should go to the depot, my wife. One day the police will come and chase you if you sell on the street."

"Why?" she said. "People like to see me at that place. It is easy for them; they know my stuff is good, fresh. The police are there to catch thieves, bad people. Not me." Zingozi knew that his mother was very determined; it had been she who had encouraged his father to take this big step and had kept him cheerful and willing during the long weeks while they dug the ditch and made the water furrow. She had borrowed money from her mother, the one Zingozi stayed with, and repaid most of it.

But her husband frowned and fidgeted. "There are rules. I don't know what they are, only we have been told to take our garden stuff to the depot. Except when we sell here, from the garden."

"We sell here without the police. Why not in Lusaka?"

"It is different. We are poor people, we cannot understand. But we must do what the President says. If he says so, we must send to the depot."

"I have not heard him say it."

"Well, it must have been so. If we had a radio we might hear. One day we'll get a radio and you, Zingozi, when you take in that sugar cane on Saturday, you go to the depot."

"But vegetable boys are all selling sugar cane in the streets," his mother said, "and those police go by. There is no trouble."

"Give me more stew," his father said, "and more tea," closing the argument.

2. Going to town

EARLY, EARLY, WHILE it was still cool and the birds were moving and twittering in the branches, Zingozi walked to the Saturday truck. When he came back at the weekend, his father almost always sent him in to Lusaka with produce to sell. When he went back to his grandmother on Sunday evening he would have another load to carry, for her; one day, he said to himself, I shall get a bicycle – one day!

He had just as many sugar canes as he could carry and a heavy knife. He cut bits for the driver and the others in the truck; they peeled off the outside with knives or teeth, chewed and spat over the side. Everyone was cheerful, bumping along, driving slow. They all had business in Lusaka. They would come back with money or else with some-

thing they wanted: tea, milk powder, nails, lamp oil, perhaps a spoon or a plastic bowl or even a pair of shoes.

At first there was bush and old fields. There was so much land to spare in Zambia, land to use if there was someone to use it. Chunga had been like that, a bit of dry nothing, till the irrigation water came and the gardens began to grow green. The truck crossed the bridge and the road got a little better; there were houses and fruit trees and bright coloured creepers. Then they could see high buildings, shops, offices. People got out here and there. Three women had big sacks from their husbands' gardens; cabbage and squash, baskets of tomatoes, green peppers, spinach, small mangoes, a heavy sweet smell. But it was now getting into the rainy season and vegetables were dropping off. They were taking theirs to the depot.

But not Zingozi. He slipped off with his bundles of cane and went over to one of the roundabout crossings a little way from the centre, where there were shops, cars coming

and going or stopping, and three good
friends he had made when he had taken
sugar cane in before. It was not his mother's
pitch; if it had been, someone might have
told her that he was there. Now he shouted to

his friends, "Hi Malenga! Hi Kupaso! Hi Tiger Boy!" And they shouted back. They were all vegetable boys, though some of them sold matches as a side-line; they were all older than he was, but not much.

There was also a much older man who hobbled over to greet Zingozi and offer him a sticky sweet. He was a little lame and some people made fun of him, but not the vegetable boys. He cleaned shoes and touched them up, making them blue or red or brown or black – at any rate for a short time. His name was Mr. Swongilse; it was said that once he had been a strong man and a good singer.

Often the vegetable boys had fresher and nicer things than the shops. Tiger Boy was big and tough, everyone knew him. He joked with all his customers, whoever they were. He told Zingozi where to stand, a little way off under a big flowering tree, with his heap of canes and his strong knife. And soon Zingozi was selling fast, putting the small coins into a bag tied onto his belt, two ngwee

bits mostly. Once he had to give change out of a kwacha note; that was better than doing it as a school sum, but he had to count twice over. Still he got it right, at least the customer thought so and that was what mattered.

Kupaso strolled over. "They say the police are getting angry with us vegetable boys."

"Why? We don't do anything wrong," said Zingozi, worried.

"The shops could be jealous with us doing

so well. But you follow whatever we do. Tiger Boy will see us right."

Zingozi began to half wish he had gone to the depot, even though the lorry driver had said they weren't taking any more cane. But if he got into police trouble, what would his father say? He looked all round; he was in the shade of a jacaranda tree; the bluey-mauve flowers had fallen every day onto the red ground, making a nice colour, kind to the eyes.

Two or three white children came over for sugar cane, but they spoke Chinyanga to him. He remembered from school and said "Good Night" to them, in real English, politely. One of them laughed. But surely he had the word right?

Then, all of a sudden, there was the loud noise of a horse trotting, cutting into all the talk and whirring of cars going fast or slow. It was a policeman on a police-horse and he rode this great brown horse up to Kumaso and pointed at his basket and shouted to him to be off. Kumaso was frightened. He

grabbed at his money box and vegetables. The policeman knocked over one basket and the big horse put a hoof onto the path and made a grab at a cabbage. A beautiful shining egg-fruit rolled out of the basket under the horse's hoofs. There was a shout from Tiger Boy and a tomato hit the horse right over its eye. Tomatoes don't hurt, especially very ripe ones, but the horse threw up its head and all of a sudden it was in the middle of a shower of tomatoes. All the vegetable boys joined in and a few other boys, seeing tomatoes lying, picked them up and had a shot at the enemy. Zingozi didn't have any tomatoes, but he threw a piece of sugar cane, pointed end first, as though it had been a spear.

The horse did not like that! The policeman pulled at the reins and tried to wipe a tomato off his own face and the horse bolted. It galloped off up the road and the boys rushed after it, trying long shots with tomatoes. Most people laughed and sympathised with the boys because nobody likes a policeman unless there's a thief in the house, when of course they want him very much. And it was clear that the boys were doing no harm, but were, in fact, providing a service to the public, and they were sorry for Kumaso whose vegetables had been spoilt. One of the men from the garage said to him: "It would be cheaper for you to get a hawker's licence because then the police would leave you alone."

"How would I get that?" asked Kumaso.

"Well, you would go to the police office in the centre and ask for a form, fill it in –"

"Oh, what are you saying! I couldn't do that. They would never give me one. Filling up forms – me! You're joking."

Mr. Swongilse came up to them. "Oh boys, you have done a foolish thing. The police will come back and revenge their comrade. He has been made to look foolish and that is the worst thing of all. Now you must expect a big attack. And you –," he said to Zingozi, "– they will say you threw a spear at the horse. If it had hit the horse's eye it might have blinded him. Or the man."

"But I did not throw at his eye, only at the fat part of his body!"

"You cannot prove that."

"Should I go away quickly?" Zingozi asked anxiously. "Must I hide?"

"No, you must stay with the others."

3. *The Vegetable War*

THE MORNING WENT on, hot, hot. There were fewer customers. Zingozi yawned and his eyes began to feel heavy, tired of light and people. He moved back close against a jacaranda tree, where there was loose dust and a little grass. He pushed his knife well under the cane stalks and his coat over all that, and stretched out. It wasn't the best of beds, but his eyes could shut. He could let go. It was good.

He woke up thirsty, but there was a tap where he could drink at the garage. He got some bread, too old to sell but good enough, from the shop. It would do till he got home. One thing about this place, there were always bits of reading lying about, old papers, things to buy, names of movies. Pictures sometimes. Guns, horses, battles!

Better than old school reading books. He
went to sleep again.

Tiger Boy woke him. "Listen, I've got a
plan. About the police. I've got a hunch they
could come soon, this afternoon. They are
bound to chase us now! Listen to this. We
run away. They take our stuff and put it in

the police car, then one of us runs really fast, between the houses, not along the road, with all the police chasing him! When they're all away, we get back our baskets, boxes, everything out of the police car and hide them. Then we will get them back in time for the afternoon sales."

"But where will we hide them?" said Zingozi, bewildered.

"Behind old sheds, doors, bushes, any-where. Cover up the boxes, pretend they are nothing – old ones, thrown away."

Kumaso had joined up with them. "I know! Put all the boxes into that store behind the big shop. Who's to look through all supermarket empties? There are a hundred places we can hide them!"

"Good idea, Kumaso. You be my Prime Minister!" And so it was all worked out. Zingozi was a little frightened, but surely Tiger Boy would win?

Now as the afternoon went on, it seemed to get hotter. And suddenly – the noise police cars make. It was scaring! Down came a big police truck like a wind, and outjumped six policemen who all ran for it, dodging behind walls and bushes. It was amazing how many narrow paths there were, in and out, behind the big houses and gardens. Two of the police seized the boys' boxes and baskets, their money boxes even, and the little tables and stools some had. They piled them into the truck then joined in the chase, shouting orders. Kumaso let himself get into sight, then ran round the church, across the graves, and jumped the wall with the police close behind him. They thought they'd got him as he led them through the old brick works. Every policeman joined in. But what was going on behind? Tiger Boy had been hiding in the old store at the back of the supermarket, close to the police truck. He and Molema and two of the others pulled out the boxes and baskets, ran back with them to the store and pushed them in behind the old empties. Then they seemed to vanish.

Zingozi was small fry compared with the other boys. He managed to climb a tree and

get hidden. But he dropped down to help Tiger Boy get the stuff out of the truck. It was great, that!

Back came the police. They had been running and running. They were hot and angry, the officer especially, and the vegetable boys had got away again. When they found the truck empty they turned on anyone who was there. "You could have stopped them! Why not? Why not? Where did they go? Who was there?" But people said they'd only just come, they hadn't seen. Some pointed one way, some another. One of the policemen seized on Zingozi who hadn't run because he didn't know the paths and ditches and broken fences behind the smart houses and shops. "You," they said, "you selling sugar cane! It's wrong, wrong! You are breaking the law!" And one of them gave him a cuff.

"Sorry, sir, sorry, I didn't know," said Zingozi sniffling.

"I bet you did," said the police officer. "I bet you know as well as the big ones! They're friends of yours, yes? Where are they?"

Zingozi shook his head and tears began coming out of the corners of his eyes. "They are not my friends," he said. It felt nasty to say that but what else could he say?

"Ah, drop him!" said the officer. "He's only a kid." And then he marched up to Mr. Swongilse, sitting there quietly on the edge of the grass, with his tins and bottles of shoe polish and shoe dye. "What have we here?" said the police officer. "Show me your licence."

But poor Mr. Swongilse only smiled and threw out his hands, empty.

"He is a very useful man," said someone in the little crowd that had gathered to see what the police would do.

"Do your duty," said the officer and his men pounced on Mr. Swongilse. They took his box and began to throw everything onto the ground. They stamped on his tins and began to break the bottles on the stones. All poor Mr. Swongilse's business dyeing the dust! Out of the shop ran an angry lady who dropped her shopping basket and caught the police officer by the arm. "Tell your men to stop breaking glass! This is where the children play. It will cut their feet!" You could see she was near to smacking the face

of one of the policemen.

The police officer was upset – he should have thought of that himself. "Take those bottles to the truck!" he said. "Stop breaking them. And you –" he turned on Mr. Swongilse "– name and address?"

"Poor man," said one of the crowd, "but Madam has saved some of his bottles, perhaps he will get them back."

"Yes," said another, "that is humanism, to help others. After he has paid his fine we shall see him again."

42

The police truck left, but without the vegetable boys' boxes and baskets, except for one stool and some squashed fruit and vegetables. One by one the boys came back, went round to the store, collected their stuff, and settled down again. Trade was brisk because now there was so much to talk about; everyone wanted to discuss the past, present and future, most of all with Tiger Boy, who had hidden under a pile of old tyres. Some of them warned him that the Government felt it was not modern, not tidy, to have vegetable sellers. All the men and women who had sold things along the streets in the middle of Lusaka had been thrown out. It was not only the police. It was the Ministers. It was the Town Council of Lusaka. Perhaps it was even the President!

"But," said Tiger Boy, "we provide a service." And this could not be denied.

Just then there was a great roaring and down the straight bit of road came a crowd of cars and motor bikes, racing. People pulled back along the paths and pavements, women

44

dragged their small ones out of harm's way and screamed, for it looked as if there must be an accident. But no, not this time. The cars roared round the poor old roundabout on two wheels and the girls beside the drivers screeched and waved. Then they roared back up the straight again.

The garage man scowled after them. "One day there's going to be a big smash-up. One child was hurt last week but not badly and the driver gave money. Next time it will be a death, sure, sure. What's more, I know

45

two or three have taken out their Dad's cars though they are under age, and have no driving licence. They'll kill one another or worse, kill one of us."

Zingozi was standing by. "What's to be done, then?"

"Every Saturday they come, about now. There is only one thing to do. Get the police."

4. Chunga Sunday

ZINGOZI SLEPT LATE on Sunday mornings, the blanket over his ears. What an exciting Saturday it had been! But he hadn't told his father and mother about it. When he handed in the bag of money his father had said gloomily. "I think you did not go to the depot."

"I heard they do not want to take sugar cane. There is no use going."

His father shook his head, did not answer that. He only said "Nobody can say what they want in the city. We are only poor people."

When he woke there was a gorgeous smell of cooking. His mother was busy. Little Kangwa was still trying to make a wire truck, sitting on the ground, dribbling with the effort. Zingozi picked up the tangle of

wire and began working on it while Kangwa watched. In a while he had got the shape. Now he needed wheels. He looked round for four tins the same size or almost. There were three the same. Kangwa came with another, but the wrong size. It was Jelita who came with a right one. Maybe he'd let her pull the truck when it was finished.

While he worked at it, he half heard his father and mother talking. They were planning to build a square house, not thatched, but with a roof of modern corrugated iron. They could get a grant for that. A metal roof is hotter, the sun beats on it, but people think it is more modern and that it looks better than thatch. Certainly it lasts

longer. But the best thing is, it catches the rain, so, if you have a tank or even a bucket, you can always get a drink of water. It would be nice to have a real house, two rooms, instead of the small, old mud-plaster house with a tiny outside kitchen that was all smoke. There could be a wide cement step, in the shade, good for sitting, talking to guests. There were several such houses now in Chunga. If they got the loan they would buy two windows and a locking door. Zingozi's father would build with sun-dried bricks. Zingozi must help build in his school holidays. Yes, he'd been afraid they'd say that! It must be done before next sowing season.

But the family had some dry land for crops as well as their garden. All the Chunga people had a patch of dry land, an acre or two on the higher ground that could not be irrigated but depended on rain. They would hire a pair of oxen and plough it. There was seed from last year.

Sometimes, now, Zingozi was half consulted over some decision about what to grow and when to plant. When this happened he felt he was a man. His father grumbled away about the work they had all agreed to do together, all the Chunga farmers (working together for everyone). This took place on Tuesdays. On a Tuesday they mended the water furrow or the road, or else they worked in the wheat fields, sowing, weeding, harvesting, cutting off the ears of wheat with a curved knife. The men beat the cut ears with sticks to loosen the grain and the women husked the wheat, then it was sold, and with the money the Chunga farmers had decided to buy a small tractor. That was the elected committee's decision. It would certainly be very useful, but who would look after it? Anyone? No-one? That had not yet been settled.

Everyone grumbled a little about the Tuesday work, but that was part of the way things were. Once Zingozi asked his father. "Is it better here than in Lusaka? Would you go back?"

51

His father thought for a time and said. "It is better here. I work and work, but I see what I do. I get it back. It is goodness, out of the ground. In Lusaka the work was not so hard, but I did not see anything, except sometimes a little money."

"But money," said Zingozi, puzzled, "that is what you get in the end. Why you sell. Why you grow – all this. Why you work."

"Not only," said his father and left Zingozi to think about it.

There, now the wire truck was finished! Zingozi put on another long and stiff wire, with a twist on it to make a handle. He ran it up and down. Then Kangwa ran it up and down. At last he remembered Jelita and gave her a turn.

Then it was dinner, a good stew with peppers out of the garden and of course cabbage. But best there were green mealies, not the ten ngwee ones, but good enough! One could chew away at them and always get a little bit more. Jelita had picked some

ripe little black mulberries from the tips of the twigs. There was tea with plenty of sugar.

"When we have our new house we will sit outside it; we will have nice painted chairs, ferns growing in tins. I must start to keep big tins; we will paint them," his mother said. And then, "Oh, it is nice to plan what we will have for our home – if one has a good husband." And she looked in a warm way at Zingozi's father.

Local people came in the afternoon and bought a few carrots, beets or leeks, leaves of chard or green beans. A man on a bicycle with a big sack took all the pawpaws which were ripe or nearly ripe. "When we have our house," Zingozi's mother said, a little crossly, "I shall plant a pawpaw just for ourselves."

In the late afternoon Zingozi was loaded up with presents for his grandmother — mostly cabbages! That finished a row. Most likely she might sell one or two. He took his school reading book but thought to himself that none of the stories in the book was as exciting as the last Saturday he'd had in Lusaka with the big boys. And then he thought about the racing cars and bikes and what the garage man had said.

Why were some people allowed to be like this? If they took their father's cars would they get a beating when they got home? Somehow he didn't think so. They were rich, they could do what they liked. Or could they? In school there were lessons about humanism. Big pictures of Kaunda. He said, "We are all humanists in Zambia." Was it being a humanist to race cars and maybe kill someone? No. And poor Mr. Swongilse, would he still be there next Saturday? Or in prison? There was all this to be thought about all along the road to Matero where the lights were going on cheerfully in the little houses he passed on the way to his grandmother.

5. Thief!

IT WAS THE usual dreary school week, learning things that didn't seem to fit into real life. In every class room the photographs of the President smiled down on them. But what did he think about what the police were doing? How was Government made? He tried to ask but wasn't told. So it went on until Friday afternoon when he went back home.

His father had heard something about the vegetable boys, perhaps read it in the papers. "Is this where you were?" he asked. "Do you know these boys who fought the police?"

"I was near," admitted Zingozi, "but perhaps it was not altogether like the papers said."

"Police trouble is always bad," said his father. "Keep away from it."

On Saturday there was another load of sugar cane to take in, and also the clock. This was a big alarm clock; it had been given to Zingozi's father instead of wages when the shop where he was working closed down. It had gone all right if you remembered to put it forward an hour every week-end, for it always lost that much.

Now it had altogether stopped. Zingozi must take it in to Mr. Aziz, the Indian shop by the market. They might be able to mend it. He must do this first, before selling his cane. It would be an extra walk, but maybe he could sell his sugar cane near the shop.

He got off the truck and managed to get the bundle of canes onto his back, steadying it with one hand while the other held the clock. At the shop he had to wait while older people were served. He looked round at all the things on the shelves, torches, door handles, knives and scissors, screw-drivers, shaving mirrors, frying pans, lamps – what a lot one could buy if one had the money. There were a lot of advertisements to read

and people to look at, some buying things
and paying for them. He specially liked a
large lady in a bright yellow dress with red
and green elephants all over it, a jingly

58

necklace and gold ear-rings as well as a lot of gold, smiling teeth. She was buying a thermos jug and couldn't decide which she liked best. But at last Zingozi was able to hand over the clock. Mr. Aziz behind the counter took the clock, unfastened its back part and looked. He wasn't sure; he might have a spare part. But it looked old. Zingozi must come back that evening.

That was good, he thought. He would have got rid of the sugar cane by then. He picked it up again, this time under one arm, balanced with the other, and walked out of the shop. Then, behind him, from the shop, came a scream and shouts of "Thief! Thief!" and out tore a big boy with a snatched hand bag which he quickly passed to another boy who ran straight towards Zingozi. The boys ran like lightning, zig-zagging through the people on the pavements who were all too surprised to stop him. But Zingozi slung the bundle of sugar cane right in his way. Down he came on his face and two or three men grabbed and held him, began hitting him

and shouting "Police, police!" The first boy
had disappeared completely.

Zingozi picked up the bag and took it
back to the shop. It belonged to the lady in
the yellow dress and she gave him a great
hug which he didn't like very much; she had

a funny smell like flowers but not very nice flowers. However, she fished in her bag and gave him a shining fifty ngwee piece; he thanked her and went out to pick up his sugar cane which had become scattered about. Someone had even run away with a piece. Three men were holding the boy who had stolen the bag and every now and then hitting him when he tried to get away. Another man was trying to find a policeman. Zingozi watched and was a little sorry for the boy, but not very. At last a policeman came; he put handcuffs on the boy and made him walk slowly. The boy's nose was bleeding where he had been hit and he was saying it was not him but the other boy. Zingozi wondered if he would be put in prison and he looked at the shining handcuffs and wondered again, would they have done that to Tiger Boy if they had caught him?

On his way to the roundabout he stopped two or three times and sold some bits of cane. And what about the fifty ngwee? Ought he to give it to his father to help with the new

house? Well, not all. He would certainly buy a bag of crisps for his friends at the round-about and perhaps a packet of sucking sweets for Kangwa and Jelita. Or biscuits? Anyhow he would go into the super-market to buy! He would watch the prices and not spend it all. But first he must settle down under his tree. The petals were still falling, still sweet. There were always more and more flowering trees. It seemed a long way from the thief and the handcuffs.

He had greeted his friends with a wave, but without talking to them yet. All were busy and there were no signs of worry. Only, was Mr. Swongilse there? He might be round the corner or even in another place.

Zingozi sold half his sugar cane before Tiger Boy came over. "Guess what!" he said. But Zingozi couldn't guess. He began to guess silly things like mice falling out of the sky. Kapaso and Molenga came over too. "Guess what!" they all said. Zingozi gave up.

Tiger Boy said very solemnly: "You've

63

got to believe me. I have a hawker's licence. A real true licence. You don't believe me? Here, see.'' He half took an envelope from his pocket; it had printing on it and that sign that meant Zambia.

"But why?" asked Zingozi. He couldn't somehow connect Tiger Boy with a licence.

"No police trouble now," said Tiger Boy.

"But you won! You won easy."

"You can't win every time. They'd get wise to what to do. So now I'm all right. Man with licence! It was easy. All I did was sign this old form. When they saw I meant it and had money ready, one police chap wrote in it for me, so all I did was pay and sign!" Tiger Boy was so excited he did little dance steps all the time.

"But the others?" Zingozi asked, "Molenga, Kumaso, Masiye, Sapi? How is it for them?"

"All fixed," said Tiger Boy. "All fixed good. All them are my employees!"

"Police believe that? No!"

"For now, they believe it. Maybe later we'll need more licences. Or more dodging! But not yet."

Kumaso said, "Tiger Boy always said we are his Cabinet; me, I am Prime Minister. It's like that now, only we've changed our name. Employees, we get called. Same thing."

"And me," asked Zingozi, "can I be employee, on Saturdays only?"

"Sure thing," said Tiger Boy and everyone had a good laugh.

6. Old songs

IT WAS NICE for Zingozi to go into the super-
market, and buy crisps and salt nuts out of
his own money and to count the change.
Then he was able to take round the crisps
and tell everyone about the thief. He told the
garage man too. "You see," said the man,
"the police are needed in a big city. A few
years back a person might go around Lusaka
any time and not get robbed. Now it gets
worse. These boys come in from the villages,
they don't want to grow crops, hoeing is too
hard work for them. They only want easy
money. And thieving is easy – when you get
away."

"I was half sorry for him," said Zingozi.

"Don't you be that," said the garage man.
"Keep being sorry for the ones that come in

looking for work, that don't get work and don't steal."

"The other one got away," Zingozi said thoughtfully.

"Maybe not for always. And you boys watch this evening when the crazy crowd comes."

Zingozi's customers dropped off in the hot time, so he was able to sleep. He had noticed that pineapples were going well. Could he say to his father that it would be good to try a few plants? All kinds of fruits grew in Zambia, and always grew quick. His father had planted banana shoots in a small wet patch in his garden and the next year there were bananas, and more the year after. Some gardens had orange trees. There was talk of growing rice in the big low-lying bit which would flood easily. Zambian rice. Zambian fruits. Lucky Zambia! All this came, mixed into his dreams. He only woke when some customers shook him.

There were two customers and behind them was an old friend, Mr. Swongilse.

Zingozi jumped up to meet him. "Greetings, Mr. Swongilse! What has happened to you? What did they do?"

Mr. Swongilse smiled slowly. "Greetings, seller of sweet cane! Well, it was not so bad, seeing I am alive and here. But I had to go to the police office and pay my fine. They gave me back the box and those things which were not broken. But they also said that if I was to use them I must pay for a licence. But where could I get the money?"

By now two or three others were listening, among them was Molenga, carrying his basket of oranges and small, sweet bananas, good ones. "Go on!" said Zingozi.

"Sir," I said to the chief policeman, "since I have paid your fine without argument, will you give me leave to work without a licence, until I have earned the big sum for a licence?"

"And what did they say?"

"They said 'No', indeed they laughed at me, younger men than I am. I said I was lame, could not do hard work, could only

pick up a little money, enough to eat. I had never done a crime, never stolen, never even struck in anger since I was a boy. Still they were hard, saying it was a rule, the Government had said. I asked if it was humanist to treat an old man so unkindly, but again they told me it was a rule and could not be broken. So I went away slowly and sad."

"That was hard!" said Zingozi. "How did you live?"

"Well, it was not as bad as it seemed and perhaps God was looking my way, for one of the policemen came after me. I was afraid but he said he had good news. There was someone in a big house who wanted a night watchman, a man of good character, not a spirits drinker, who could stay awake at nights. 'Are you this man?' the policeman asked me, and I said that I was."

"Ah," said Zingozi, "so perhaps this was humanist after all, to be kind and think of others!"

"He went with me to the house and said that I was the man for the job, and that is

where I am today. But my story is not over.
Last night, that is, Friday night, I was
walking round the wall of this big house,
carrying a stick which had been given to me
and sometimes beating at a thick bush. And,

so as to keep myself awake, I started to sing
an old song. You have never heard me sing,
Zingozi, for I only know the old songs and
not these ones that come out of boxes, nor
yet the songs you young ones learn in the

schools. Well, then, I was singing to myself. Once indeed, long ago, my voice was powerful, I was known as a singer. But as a man gets older, the power goes."

"And then?"

"The man whose house I was guarding came out, with a beer mug in each hand. He passed one to me and told me to sing again. He asked for another song, an old one, and yet another. We drank beer together while I sang and he told me stories which I did not know or had forgotten. It was as though we were old friends. Before that I had scarcely seen him. He had been a stranger. Now we are known to each other. As I still had a few of my tins and bottles I cleaned his shoes, free."

That was a story full of good luck, thought Zingozi, in spite of the unkindness of the police. He cut a big piece of sugar cane and gave it to Mr. Swongilse. Molenga gave him two bananas. "Where do you sleep?" asked Zingozi.

"At the house of this man, on a blanket in

a corner of the garden. It is a garden with many trees, some fruit trees; there is a machine which cuts grass and a stone bird."

"Why is there a stone bird?"

"I think that is because this man likes to look at it and stroke it with his hands. Who knows? Now I will go back to sleep and try to remember more of the old songs."

"Well," said Molenga, "that was Mr. Swongilse's lucky day when the police came, though we did not know it. There is now a new man who sells baskets and little wooden animals. I think he comes from among those ones who used to sell in the big street before the police came. They have to live."

"I think it is funny that Tiger Boy has this licence," said Zingozi, "but perhaps it is sensible. It is a nice feeling to have a war, but not for too long."

"He has put up prices a little to pay for it," Molenga said. "Now he is not afraid if people complain."

"Ah, that makes sense," said Zingozi.

7. *They had it coming*

THE GARAGE MAN strolled over to Zingozi. "Come," he said. "Watch!"

Zingozi and most of the others went over near the garage. A police van was drawn up by the road. At the far side there were more. What was going to happen?

Further up the road the racket was beginning and now, down it came, that racing roar, worse than ever! But the police van had moved out, blocking the cars. Other police had held up the traffic going past the roundabout until this thing was cleared up. A couple of cars dodged the police van and dashed through, but they were held up at the block. Now there was a great jumble of cars, motor bikes, men and boys shouting, police whistles. Three of the cars, going too fast, had collided. One had skidded off the road

and turned over. The boy who had been
driving crawled out – the garage man had
run to help him, but he was only a little cut.
He was lucky the car had not caught on fire.

But there were crumpled mudguards, big scratches on the cars, girls with torn dresses and scattered handbags. It was a sight!

Zingozi watched. The police were going

from one to the other, taking notes, writing in their books. "See," said the garage man, "no licence!"

Then one of them, a boy in a smart suit, striped shirt, gold wrist watch, hit one of the policemen. Out came the handcuffs. Zingozi gasped. A girl screamed and made to attack the policeman, but another held her back. "What will they do?" Zingozi asked the garage man in a whisper.

"They will be charged in court. Look, their names and addresses are in the books. One has a father who is High-Up, always making speeches. He does not know what his son is up to, he will get a big surprise! All these will have to go into court. They will have to pay big fines. Or their fathers will. And they will have a big talking-to by the judge. They will hang their heads."

A few had been let go. They had not been driving dangerously. These had mostly been at the back. Two were ordinary drivers, one man and one lady; both had their licences and had not been drinking. Most of the young ones had been drinking.

There was a crowd now; many of them had been frightened by the racing cars earlier on. Some of them shouted at the drivers or shook their fists. The car block at the roundabout was lifted; the drivers whose names had been taken, but who had licences, were allowed to go on, but the ones without licences were told to walk. Policemen got into their cars and drove them away. One of the young men sat down beside the road and cried; a girl sat down next to him and she began crying too. The car which had skidded was still there on its side. Two others and a bike had to be taken into the garage. "Good business for me!" said the garage man, and laughed. Then he went over and offered to drive home those whose cars had been taken. "They are not going to quarrel over the price!" the garage man added.

Tiger Boy shook his head. "Like it is written in the Bible; how are the mighty fallen!" He had some beautiful juicy pine-apples; that morning he had gone early to the main market and had bought them for three ngwee each more than the grower had been paid and sold them for another ten ngwee above that. He would sell them all by the evening. Now Tiger Boy took some of the pineapples round to the young folk who had been in trouble. He offered them sympathetically, cutting them up nicely there and then. Kapaso offered halved oranges. The young ones were pleased; it was something to take their minds off it and they didn't care if they paid a few ngwee extra.

Gradually the crowd melted away. Zingozi had sold almost all his sugar cane. The sun was in the tops of the trees, beginning to drop. And suddenly he remembered the clock, he must hurry! He gave the rest of the sugar cane to Molenga and Kupaso. If they sold it, good and well. Then he set off for the centre of town. He must get to the shop, and then to the truck.

He was panting when he got to the shop. "I've come for the clock, Mr. Aziz," he said.

Mr. Aziz took the clock out of a drawer.

"Look, son, I went through this clock's insides, but it was no use. This clock is an old lady, she can't work, she should be in her grave, buried."

Zingozi felt very sad. "What will they say at home! Our clock!"

"Never you mind," said Mr. Aziz, "you are the boy who stopped the thief, right? Now, that was good. Good for me. If people say there was a thief stole a handbag in Mr. Aziz's shop, then they don't come. Now they do come, they want to hear the story and I tell them and mostly they stop and buy. So I give you a clock, a young clock. Look, it has a blue face and red hands, it is a very smart clock. It goes well, better than the old one. Take it, boy, take it. It is a present from me because you are a brave boy."

Zingozi took it in his hands. He had no words, only the smile spread round his face and he looked at Mr. Aziz and Mr. Aziz had a big smile too. They wrapped the new clock in pink paper. Then Mr. Aziz began to shut up his shop and Zingozi helped with the

shutters. It was all so good! Yes, he knew he was a brave boy and if there was another vegetable war he would be Tiger Boy's top General and they would be sure to win; already he was thinking of a new plan! And meanwhile, think what he would have to tell everybody, first in the truck and then back at Chunga!